I0640582

Firebrand

Firestorm

The Ancestors of Bjorn Esterday

Volume 02

Perseverance

March 1776

Wynter Sommers

Wynter Sommers

Published by Pure Force Enterprises, Inc.
California, USA
Since 2002

INGRAM

INGRAM® Distribution

DEDICATION

To those who feel strongly about truth, justice, and the integrity of America; your honorable actions make us proud. To those who wonder if their daily choices matter; your small decisions impact generations to come. To those everyday people who don't think they have what it takes; when you strive for extraordinary things, the impossible becomes reality. Your dreams today become our future tomorrow. Thank you for everything you do.

Bjorn Esterday
Was Not Born Yesterday
Series

Firebrand (15 Volumes+Conversation Station Book)
Edges (9 Stories +Conversation Station Book)
Gone (18 Stories + Conversation Station Book)

Bjorn EDGES Series

EDGES Book 1-Swift Encounter
EDGES Book 2-Rousing Attack
EDGES Book 3-One Foot Under
EDGES Book 4-Earthshake
EDGES Book 5-Broken String
EDGES Book 6-Key Witness
EDGES Book 7-Who is She?
EDGES Book 8-Vanish
EDGES Book 9-Chase or Die

Bjorn Series Alternate Reading Plan

1st	Edges Book 1
2nd	Edges Book 2
3rd	Gone Book 1
4th	Firebrand Vol 1
5th	Edges Book 3
6th	Firebrand Vol 2
7th	Gone Book 2
8th	Gone Book 3
9th	Firebrand Vol 3
10th	Gone Book 4
11th	Firebrand Vol 4
12th	Gone Book 5
13th	Gone Book 6
14th	Edges Book 4
15th	Firebrand Vol 5
16th	Gone Book 7
17th	Firebrand Vol 6
18th	Gone Book 8
19th	Firebrand Vol 7
20th	Gone Book 9
21st	Firebrand Vol 8

22nd	Gone Book 10
23rd	Firebrand Vol 9
24rd	Gone Book 11
25th	Firebrand Vol 10
26th	Gone Book 12
27th	Gone Book 13
28th	Firebrand Vol 11
29th	Gone Book 14
30th	Firebrand Vol 12
31st	Gone Book 15
32nd	Firebrand Vol 13
33rd	Gone Book 16
34th	Firebrand Vol 14
35th	Gone Book 17
36th	Firebrand Vol15 (End)
37th	Gone Book 18 (End)
38th	Edges Book 5
39th	Edges Book 6
40th	Edges Book 7
41st	Edges Book 8
42nd	Edges Book 9(End)

ACKNOWLEDGMENTS

We acknowledge those who actively build peace. We acknowledge all the selfless talent which contributed to creating meaningful tokens of consideration and sharing. We acknowledge that every person has a daily choice of right or wrong... and we thank you for choosing the right, good, honorable path filled with integrity because that is the difficult and brave path. Small choices today become lasting monuments of loving hope tomorrow.

CONTENTS

0 PREFACE

Last time, we saw that Jane was waiting for Tweedbottom to arrive for tea. Mr. Tweedbottom was a friendly person in these strange colonies. Jane needed friends.

Meanwhile Polly's husband, Button, told her to run...and she did, but did her husband make it out alive?

1 CHAPTER 08: (FEB 1776) Tea Time with Jane

The colonies lacked the excitement of European social interaction. Jane sometimes found the days a bit dreary, but she did look forward to the bright visits of Mr. Tweedbottom, local tailor and fashion expert.

He had met her one day as she was gazing at some fashion etchings he had in the window of his tailor shop. He realized she was new to the colony.

"Jane?" Mr. Tweedbottom asked. "How do you like this quaint village of Dover, here in the Delaware Colony? Did your uncle describe it accurately? Did it meet your expectations?"

Jane smiled, "It is quite pleasant, Mr. Tweedbottom." She started, "Uncle Floyd said he made an agreement with his Christian business partner, Mr. Tyler, to only travel to states which have synagogues. He even made me memorize the list."

"Memorize?" Mr. Tweedbottom asked, "how odd to restrict the colonies which one visits..."

"Oh, Uncle Floyd," Jane described, "was a bit miffed his brother married a Christian woman and raised me Christian, so Uncle Floyd asked that I memorize all the temples in the colonies."

"And," Mr. Tweedbottom added, "Attend, as well? I do not harken to any religion, but I envy the Jews, who are reputed to have a keen sense of business. Although your Uncle is of the middling sort, I admire the profits he makes. I shall test you. Pray, tell me the synagogues and colonies he plans to visit."

Jane looked up and recalled, "There are none here in Dover. He does plan travel for business or holidays to... Um..." Jane looked down and took a sip of tea.

"Go on," Mr. Tweedbottom prodded.

Jane nodded as she held up her hand, touched her thumb, and said, "*Congregation Mikveh Israel* is located in Philadelphia in the Pennsylvania colony." Then Jane touched her ring finger and announced, "*Touro Synagogue* is located in Newport in the Rhode Island Colony. *Kahal Kadosh Beth Elohim* Synagogue is in Charleston in the South Carolina Colony." Jane paused as she was now pinching her ring finger and thought, then said, "Oh! *Congregation Shearith Israel* is in the New York Colony."

"Ah, yes, I have been to the New York Colony for my business," Mr. Tweedbottom said. "When you visit this colony, you will note it is rather large. There is a section of New York called *the Manhattan* and I believe that synagogue is situated in the upper portions of the Western Side." He leaned forward to add, "Is that every place he would visit in the thirteen colonies?"

Jane shook her head, "One more that I know of. There are more, I'm sure, but the only remaining one is in the Colony of Georgia. In a place called Savannah. I think it is called the *Congregation Mickve of Israel* ."

Mr. Tweedbottom hunched over the table and gazed into Jane's eyes, whispering, "I admire any woman who has the intelligence to list a set of buildings she has never been to. I find it very attractive. Almost as attractive as

Venetian lace."

This was not London, where she could hide in the crowd if she chose to. Jane accepted the flirtatious comments of Mr. Tweedbottom.

Jane replied, "I am uncertain if I should take that as a compliment, or rebuff you for being too forward in your intentions, Mr. Tweedbottom." She paused, "Or was that a sly insult equating my ability to list buildings as possessing the same intellect as a bit of fabric?"

Mr. Tweedbottom challenged, "I speak only in jest, Miss Hargreaves." Then Mr. Tweedbottom smirked, "Are you not able to laugh at yourself? I did not equate your intellect with fabric."

It was said Mr. Tweedbottom could make ball gowns out of scraps, yet that publicity came mostly from Mr. Tweedbottom himself, but his pompous self-aggrandizement amused Jane. She would have to ignore his comments, as she was hopeful that if they did become close friends, such guised insults would soon fade as he learned to admire and appreciate her qualities. She had never actually seen one of his finished gowns, but she was sure he was probably the finest in this colony. He probably did not compare to other tailors or dress makers in London, but Jane could not be particular about dressmakers, nor possible future husbands as she was getting beyond the age of a bride, per society's opinion. Out here in these rugged colonies, Jane's fashion standards and her romance standards might slip a bit. She had few options.

Jane sighed.

No more would she plan trips to Venice and order *point de Venise a reseau* lace for her dresses. Nor would she go to the isle of *Burano*, just an hour by gondola from Venice, to purchase their distinct style of lace. Oh, the Italians knew how to take a needle and create crisp white laces. Leonardo Di Vinci visited Burano in 1481 to purchase cloth for the alter at the Duomo in Milano, Italy... and since then, all gentle-folk with exquisite tastes would visit *Burano* to purchase their fabrics.

In 1665, the French created an imitation of the Italian style lace in Alençon, calling that style point d'Alençon. It was rumored the French forced twenty Venetian women to live in Alençon to teach the French the art of lace making. The French, English, and Flemish lace prices had started dropping a score of years ago, but not the Italian laces.

Although it was time consuming, lace was a profitable business as long as it remained in fashion. Would the price drop? Maybe, but it wasn't likely some inventor would create a mechanical device to actually make lace without a schooled lace maker. Perhaps with all these battles occurring here in the New World, lace would not be as important as, say food, but Jane wondered if income from lace trading was how Mr. Tweedbottom seemed to live so comfortably.

Lace. It would make sense.

Perhaps she would ask him at tea today. If he were amorous toward her, she would need to find out the state of his finances to ensure he could support her, after all...

Jane looked out her window and saw all the people going about their business of the day.

Ah, there was Mr. Tyler. Mr. Bryce Aiden Tyler. Jane didn't know Mr. Tyler was planning on visiting Uncle Floyd today. Well, they are business partners, so perhaps he doesn't need an appointment...and, therefore...

Perhaps Uncle Floyd doesn't need to tell Jane every time Mr. Tyler's magnetic personality enters his home. Uncle Floyd, after all, was oblivious to the effect Mr. Tyler had on Jane.

Oh, of course, a woman just approached Mr. Tyler in the street. Was she engaging him in conversation. Are those flowers she is holding? Absurd wilted things. Is she holding up each one by one, as if to drag out a conversation?

Jane shook her head, taking a very long and controlled breath and then with pursed lips, she looked down at the others on the street. A woman there... and there...men discussing something over on the other side...

Children playing over here... Oh, and there is Mr. Tweedbottom looking very determined. He is walking so briskly.

Jane smiled. Mr. Tweedbottom. A welcomed sight, indeed. Nice to see somebody firmly determined on his way to see her. Yes. She must be practical and realize Mr. Tweedbottom just might be suitable for her, after all.

At least this little plump self-satisfied man of discerning taste was to be her companion for tea today. It will be nice to discuss the frivolities of fashion and pass the time. Not wanting Mr. Tweedbottom to see her peering from the window, Jane stepped back and headed down stairs to the parlor.

By the time she descended, the butler Witherspoon heard a knock and opened the front door. Silversmith, her maid, immediately ran to get the biscuits warmed to serve.

Jane remained standing.

She wanted to see if Mr. Tweedbottom would notice that Silversmith had fixed her pannier and she was no longer, "lopsided", as he commented last time.

"Good afternoon, Mr. Tweedbottom," Jane started after Witherspoon had brought him into the parlor, "I'm delighted you could make it for tea."

Jane waited. Mr. Tweedbottom replied, "Miss Hargreaves. I was delighted to be invited."

11

He gave a crisp slight bow and Jane responded with the short dip of a curtsey. Mr. Tweedbottom inhaled, smelling the baked goods wafting from the kitchen, thanks to Silversmith.

"The aroma is intoxicating," Mr. Tweedbottom commented.

Jane guided him to sit at the table, already set. She was pleased he did not make any comment about her skirts, as that simply indicated that Silversmith, once again, had come through by solving a problem creatively. What would she do without Silversmith.

They were served by Witherspoon and laughed and spoke of fashion.

"Lace, especially Chantilly lace, would take a year to make a proper shawl," Mr. Tweedbottom explained, "One must order it from Europe. The colonies do not have sufficient skills to hand make lace,"

"Really," Polly asked, "Over here is lace held to such a standard?"

"Indeed," Mr. Tweedbottom replied, "In Europe and maybe eventually here, they have lace inspectors at the city gates who will determine if your lace is appropriate for your station."

"Or, if they see that you are defying convention by wearing lace which is too extravagant for you, the inspectors will cut it down to the proper width with scissors, burn it, or ask you to remove it altogether before letting you into the city."

"I suppose you have made your fortunes in lace trading," Jane commented taking a sip of tea. "Knowing so much about finery, would put you in demand in these colonies. I can imagine you are the only one who could advise a gentleman on the proper cuff or a lady needing the right accent for her gown."

Mr. Tweedbottom's eyes widened. "My fortune? Have I been ostentatious with my spending that you would make such a comment, Miss Hargreaves? I find it gauche to discuss money at tea..."

Worried she had offended him, Jane offered, "Oh, no, Mr. Tweedbottom, It's just that you know of the Italian island of Burano and the glass making sister island of Murano. You know of Chantilly, Venetian and so many other laces, I simply assumed... I mean, you always dress with aplomb...er... Your conversations interject facts on finery of which the average person would be ignorant... I mean, you give every appearance of a fine, discrete, well-bred gentleman, Mr. Tweedbottom." Jane took a deep breath and waited.

He said nothing.

"Mr. Tweedbottom," Jane added hurriedly as she stepped away from the table to pick up a fashion etching from the side table and brought it to her tea companion, "You see there, the type of lace on her handkerchief? And the buttons and bows on her bodice?" Jane stood over the seated man and showed him the picture, her lorgnette dangled from her necklace chain and accidentally bumped him in the shoulder.

Mr. Tweedbottom squinted and then looked up at Jane saying, "May I borrow your lens, Miss Hargreaves?"

"Most certainly,Mr. Tweedbottom," Jane started as she took off her necklace and handed it to the gentleman. "My cousin in England," Jane explained, "makes musical instruments and he likes to tinker and create things one cannot buy in shops. He calls this the lorgnette."

Mr. Tweedbottom examined it, then used it, "Hmph. Most definitely Italian lace," he confirmed looking at the hand colored etching, handing back the lorgnette to Jane, "Although the artist here simply implies it, but my trained eye can pick up the intent of the designer of this gown. Here are your spectacles on a stick...or chain...or what have you..."

"Could I be vulgar and ask how much you would charge me to make such a creation, including the lace, buttons and bows?" Jane flinched, hating to ask.

15

"The cost? Including my labor?" Mr. Tweedbottom asked askance, "I see we are discussing money, again."

"You see, I don't have the abundant luxuries I had back in England," Jane explained. "My allowance is already spoken for with fixed expenses, you see. I would need to save up and plan to order such a creation from your shop."

"Perhaps if you need to ask the cost, it is too early for you to consider buying a gown from me, my dear Miss Hargreaves," Mr. Tweedbottom emphasized, rubbing his eyes. "Back in '68 *John Heathcoat* invented a Bobbin net machine to make lace at a bargain. In the last seven or eight years, I'm sure he's made some improvements to allow a woman in your financial situation to purchase lace at a price you could afford here in the colonies, Miss Hargreaves."

"I don't think anything made by machine could rival the quality of handmade laces," walking back to her own seat, Jane picked up her tea cup, took a sip of tea, allowing for the cup to clink against the saucer as she walked to the window to look out. Then she glanced back at Mr. Tweedbottom who seemed to be straining to see his own pocket watch, "Your eyes, Mr. Tweedbottom?"

"Working 'til dusk with a needle and thread harms ones vision," he dismissed.

Mr. Tweedbottom got up and joined her at the window and grimaced. "You shouldn't look at that Mr. Tyler like that, my dear. What is done is done." Mr. Tweedbottom's slight double-chin jiggled as he clenched his jaw and shook his head admonishing Jane.

"Oh?" Jane didn't realize she had been so transparent as she gazed at the Mr. Bryce Aiden Tyler, the man her Uncle did business with. He was still on the street, engaged in conversation, but now another lady had joined the first. What on earth has Mr. Tyler to share with various ladies passing by holding flowers, Jane asked herself. Odd.

17

"He may be comely, but he is suspicious of character," Mr. Tweedbottom shared, "I only want to save you from being foolish, my dear. Do not be swayed by a handsome visage simply because he is gracious in manner...I hate to say it, but ..."

"But what, Mr. Tweedbottom? He is a second generation settler so rather knows these lands... Uncle Floyd trusts him..."

"Oh, my dear. I eschew gossip, but I do know that the ladies do quite fancy him," Mr. Tweedbottom pointed out the window to demonstrate his point, "and he has the most ...how do I say it...he is quick to tire of a damsel who finally gives in to him. Collects them for sport. I'm afraid he has a dubious character, which contradicts his wholesome facade. I dare say he has even been accused of living beyond his means. In debt, I hear."

"Really! I have not noticed any overt extravagances. But, you Mr. Tweedbottom, with your fancy single lens on a cord, which nobody else has... Your monocle, Mr. Tweedbottom. Don't you have it?"

"Oh, yes." Mr., Tweedbottom patted a tiny pocket on his vest. "Right here, I simply wanted to try your device for the eyes." And then he said, "I find that to enjoy entertainments, one must travel a bit."

"That is a sudden turn in our conversation, Mr. Tweedbottom." Jane laughed. "But, I also tire of speaking about Mr. Tyler. So, do share with me of which entertainments do you speak?"

"I know you loved your uncle ..." Mr. Tweedbottom said.

"Uncle Floyd, yes. Last night he said he would be too busy for tea today. He's working on something all consuming, you see. I don't know what, but he's been locked away in the library all day, " Jane dismissed.

"You can always rely on me to be your

rock, Miss Hargreaves," Mr. Tweedbottom shared.

Jane slowly looked at him, a bit perplexed, "Thank you?" she said with a slow wavering tone, uncertain how to respond.

"Well, because in town, I heard that Mr. Tyler and Mr. Hargreaves, your uncle, had a falling out." Mr. Tweedbottom shared.

"Really? I hadn't heard..." Jane was very perplexed indeed, "About what?"

"Oh, who knows," the stout man replied, "Some disagreement about who to listen to about something and not interfering."

"Ah. That clears it up," Jane commented sarcastically.

"Ladies should never worry about the business of men. The gentler sex should focus on the fashions of next season," Mr. Tweedbottom advised.

Suddenly, a shot was heard... A shot that seemed so close by

Jane stopped as Mr. Tweedbottom froze, then squinted at his pocket watch again.

Then there was a knock at the front door.

2 CHAPTER 09: (MARCH 1776) Button Nabbed

Button fought valiantly to defend his cabin, but soon his ammunition ran out. He did wound some of his attackers, but not enough to stop them from rushing into his home with hatchets, tomahawks, knives, bows and arrows.

In they swooped, showing their dominance by demolishing the furniture Button had either built or traded for.

Button was cornered by one man while he observed the others smashing things taken out from his home.

Button's shaving cloth was now snatched from Button's shoulder by the attacker guarding him. His assailant used it to bind Button's hands.

The Indian fellow shoved Button and shouted, "Slave!" Button said, "I beg your pardon?"

The man repeated as he held Button firm, "Slave!"

Then, Button saw one pile of wood, still not fully assembled. Another man smashed it to bits. This was meant to be the crib for his unborn child.

For a moment, Button exhaled sharply as if somebody had punched him in the stomach. His reaction surprised even him. He tried to focus on the fact that perhaps this band of tribal attackers did not realize it was a crib. If they did not realize it was meant for a child, then they would not need to look for a child or the child's mother. It was unlikely, but Button hoped that Polly and their unborn child escaped.

Button became a willing prisoner, hoping that his compliance would keep the attackers in his home instead of out searching for others. He was prepared to die that day to give Polly a chance to get away.

Broken and exhausted, Button surrendered and sunk to his knees.

Another Indian warrior came in after the others had secured Button and smiled.

He looked at Button and said, "English buy you. You slave." The man then spoke to the others, who seemed to be getting directions from this man.

Button did not have to know their language to understand that they needed to discuss if they would kill him or imprison him or transport him as a slave.

He was a prisoner, undoubtedly bound for slavery, as Polly had mentioned but moments earlier.

The man who spoke broken English turned to look at Button and barked once more, "Slave." And then he left.

Four men remained. They boxed Button in. One in front, one behind and one on each side. They all marched, with only Button as their prisoner.

If this was a slave raid, and if they found Polly, they would have captured her also. Wouldn't they?

There were no exact rules of protocol for this. Or maybe they saw she was with child and thought she couldn't handle the trip, so killed her. Or maybe, Button pondered...

Polly actually did escape.

There was always a chance. Polly often said one must have hope and believe in even the slimmest of chances.

The group marched away from his cabin, the home Button built with his wife, Polly.

Button, their only prisoner, estimated they had trekked for miles. He looked around, the leader, a man dressed in different tribal garb than the others, seemed to know where he was leading the group.

When Button looked around, it all was wilderness. This indiscernible blend of trees, birds, hills, meadows, rocks, brooks... it all looked the same.

During the silence, Button observed the garb of each of his captors. They all looked different, as if they were from different tribes. The leader seemed to be wearing a necklace of buttons from soldier uniforms.

Perhaps this is how this group got paid. He wondered if this band of men was comprised of members who did not fit in with their own tribes, so they sought out another occupation. One involving kidnapping of colonists, again as Polly had mentioned... and as he dismissed.

One man in front, one behind, and one to each side of him.

During those tiring miles of silence, Button noticed not all the men who attacked were in this tiny party. The others whom he wounded at his cabin must have returned to some camp to seek out their medicine man. Now Button only had four to contend with. If only he knew where he was...or where they were going. Button assumed some town with a port to ship him off to a foreign land to be enslaved...

They stopped by a small pool of water. Button was surprised to hear the leader say to him, "You drink." "Do you speak English?" Button asked him.

The leader replied, "drink!" more loudly.

Button obeyed, but with the rag still binding his wrists, Button tried to get on his knees and cup the water with his hand, bringing it up to his mouth to drink. This was not very effective, as the water would leak out before it got to his mouth. After the others laughed, one of them unbound his wrists.

Button found solace in his thoughts. His thirst was over powering. He saw the others drink.

Button wondered If somebody left England, Old World, as he did, and ventured over to the New World, would that person have insight into the overt injustices of the ultra-wealthy and their tremendous arbitrary abuses of the common man?

Button, now with unbound hands, then got down on his stomach, and using his now free hands to lower his upper body into the water, he sipped up the cool sweet refreshment.

He determined in his heart to be very obedient so they would not bind his wrists. Soon, they started walking once more.

Button wondered. Could this band of men be hired by the French? It couldn't be the English, his own people.

The French had tried to co-exist with the natives of this New Continent and made alliances with several tribes, but not all. Some chose the side of the British.

The British monarchy wanted to fiercely protect this new land. The British monarchy did not discover this place. They did not suffer the pestilence, which the first pilgrims experienced. Some didn't even have a desire to visit this great island-continent.

So, why, wondered Button, would the British want this land so much? He could only conclude that they wanted to rule this New World to extend the reach of the British Empire.

If the British wanted to extend their borders, then, Button concluded, they would need English men, like Button, to occupy these lands. It would not behoove them to hire Indians to kidnap their own kind. Polly was mistaken about the crown being behind hiring men like his captures.

Button looked around him. The birds flew overhead. It was a crisp day and if he were not held prisoner, it would have been a nice day for a picnic.

Button continued to think about who could be behind his kidnapping.

If the Crown wanted their own people settling this land, then they would also need to send Red Coats to defend the land from other countries and to keep order in the colonies. Perhaps the salary of all the Red Coats was getting too expensive.

Ah, Button thought, but again, the King of England would need his subjects to collect taxes to help pay the salaries of the Red Coats. Again, no reason to kidnap colonists.

He looked over at the leader's necklace, which glinted in the sun. Most of the buttons hanging from his necklace might be from British uniforms, but he couldn't be sure.

What could prove to be more profitable than taxing the colonists to pay for the soldier's salaries? What about the goods the British shipped to the colonists, requiring them to accept the cargo? Sometimes the quality was substandard but a shipment could not be refused. Button wondered about this.

Button had heard rumors that in 1764, the British had borrowed from banks and investors the outrageous sum of 130 million pounds.

This could buy a country.

The British shipped goods to the colonists for 885 thousand British pounds each year to cover that debt. It had been a dozen years, now... So, after twelve years, the Crown would have already collected 10,620,000 pounds.

Ten million six hundred twenty thousand. That means today, the Crown still owes over 119 million pounds in debt.

Forcing the colonists to accept the sub-standard British goods was not profitable enough to balance the King's books, Button concluded.

What other industry would be profitable? Perhaps Polly was right after all. Maybe slavery was more profitable.

Would another colonist, perhaps a neighbor, pay a tribe to steal men and women from their homes to sell to the slave traders?

Slave traders who are funded by the Crown? Could it be?

Button heard of merchants who imported tens of thousands of slaves from a land called Africa into one of the middle colonies, New York.

But, those slaves were not his

neighbors. Could it be that this trade was so profitable the British had to branch off from Africa and dip into the population of newcomers from Europe?

Button's captors had walked the entire day and now they were greeted with the setting sun.

Evidently, here is where they would make camp for Button's first night of captivity.

The four men lay out blankets on the ground. Button was roughly shoved to the ground and a blanket covered him.

Two body guards lay on either side of the blanket covering Button, pinning him down. If Button tried to escape, they would awaken instantly.

Button lay quite still on his back, staring up into the sky as the sun dimmed into a canopy of rich blues fading into ebony.

One by one, the sparkling stars shone

to contrast against the pitch of night. Button determined that he would be a star, a bright colonists shining against the black hearts who funded this kidnapping endeavor. He would make more savvy choices.

Then, he heard the men on either side of him snore...

3 CHAPTER 10: (FEB 1776) Did You Hear a Bang?

Inside the Parlor, Jane looked at Mr. Tweedbottom asking, "Did you hear a bang?" The knock on the front door came again, more urgently.

Silversmith, Jane's maid, rushed down the stairs to open the door. A second later, Silversmith rushed into the parlor breathless, "Madame, it's Mr. Tyler at the door...and ... there is something else..."

Silversmith glanced at Mr. Tweedbottom nervously as if she shouldn't speak in front of guests. "Yes, Silversmith?" Jane encouraged.

Silversmith was overshadowed by the frame of Bryce Aiden Tyler, now standing behind her. "I think Silversmith doesn't know how to tell you that I passed your Butler, Witherspoon, in the hallway. He seems to be having problems getting into your library so I may meet with your Uncle."

"Lead the way, Silversmith," Jane stood up quickly, annoyed at this Mr. Tyler and his disregard for basic etiquette by preventing Silversmith from answering Jane's question. Jane pushed past Mr. Tyler as she followed Silversmith into the hallway. Mr. Tweedbottom and Bryce Aiden Tyler followed.

Witherspoon was fumbling with all the keys on his ring holding them all and then turned to Jane explaining, "Miss. I am certain the sound came from the

Library. I was just at the writing table over there, but your Uncle is not responding and I cannot unlock this door."

Jane rapped sharply on the door, "Uncle? It is I, Jane. Uncle Floyd? Please open the door, Uncle Floyd." "I shall go outside to investigate," Mr. Tweedbottom helpfully offered.

Bryce Aiden Tyler turned to Jane, "I heard a loud bang when I was outside, yet I dismissed the possibility that it would emanate from within your household. With your permission..." Mr. Tyler swept his hand to indicate that he would try to force the door down.

"Silversmith," Jane ordered as she stepped back with a nod to Bryce, "Run and collect an authority or Magistrate if you can find him, to assist us."

Bryce tried to ram the door with his shoulder. Silversmith curtseyed and rushed out.

Bryce stepped back to hit the library door again with the weight of his body. The door was not budging.

"Miss Hargreaves, Witherspoon," Bryce Aiden Tyler asked, "Do you have tools. These seem to be hand- made Mortise or butt hinges. We can remove the pins and take the door off."

Jane nodded at Witherspoon, who rushed off and quickly returned with a chisel and hammer.

Bryce started tapping at the hinges and got one pin released. Then, the next until all pins were released from the hinges.

Then Mr. Tweedbottom returned through the front door reporting to the group, "There is no sign outside of an intruder. All the windows appear to be locked, Jane."

With the familiar reference to the Jane's Christian name, Bryce Aiden Tyler looked carefully at this Mr.

Tweedbottom with narrowing eyes.

Suddenly, Silversmith returned with three gentlemen. The magistrate, Karl Pinkney, his brother and a doctor. They helped Bryce and Witherspoon pull the door off.

When the door came off, the group fell silent. Inside, they saw the motionless body of Uncle Floyd Hargreaves at his desk, face down. Slack.

"Uncle Floyd?" Jane's voice cracked as she rushed over to him, pushing her petticoats aside to get closer to her Uncle. Then she stepped back in horror unable to look away. "I thought perhaps his heart had failed...but...."

Jane withdrew her hand to show blood on it. Her Uncle's blood.

Mr. Tweedbottom rushed to Jane. "Oh, my dear Miss Hargreaves!" He glared at Bryce Aiden Tyler, then back at Jane, "You shouldn't expose yourself to this."

Mr. Tweedbottom then wrapped his arm around a wobbly Jane. Bryce scrutinized Mr. Tweedbottom. The doctor rushed over, and confirmed Uncle Floyd Hargreaves was dead.

4 CHAPTER 11: (MARCH 1776) Button Looks Up

In the cool forest morning, Button was awakened by one of his captors. He looked up in time to see a dead rabbit being tossed at him, hitting him in the face.

A rabbit must have been trapped earlier while he slept, Button reasoned.

Another of his captors gave Button a knife, indicating that Button should start to skin the undernourished furry creature.

Button sat up, smiled and took the knife.

Next, Button sat down on the ground and watched as another man started putting stones and branches together to build a fire.

The third Indian looked up as a bird flew overhead and shot it out of the sky with his bow and arrow.

It landed to the ground with a thud. He walked over to it and picked up the bird, tossing it at the feet of Button. Then, the man mimed the action of pulling out feathers.

Perhaps this was Button's new job, to be servant to these four men. Button smiled and started working on his task.

To avoid the silence, Button looked at the leader and decided to talk. "Last month," Button shared, "a man came into the town near where the cabin is. He said he was giving the same speech in every town that would allow him to speak."

Button smiled. The leader replied with, "You drink." But there was no water around, so Button concluded that this man's grasp of English was minimal.

Button started plucking feathers from the bird as the leader stoked the fire. They were all hungry, but Button did not let his hunger show.

Button continued speaking, "He said he was practicing for a speech with the American Commissioner for Indian Affairs. Imagine that. I'm sure he would have liked to have you as his audience." Button smiled.

The leader just looked at him.

Button continued his feather plucking. "He said he would deliver it to Philadelphia later on after the speech was polished. He wanted to address newly settled colonists, like me. And Indians, like you... But ones who spoke English, no doubt."

One of the other men picked up a feather, wiped it clean and stuck it in Button's hair. The others laughed.

"I think," Button shared, "Indians who are allies to English settlers are from the tribes of *Delaware*, *Seneca*, *Munsee* and the *Mingo* ... are you from one of those tribes?"

The leader said, "You drink." And seemed satisfied that he was communicating with Button.

"Let' me see if I recall any of his speech," Button murmured as he looked down at the dead fowl in his hands. "We were all born, yet not all born evil. This trait really only belongs to a few men...

"Nay, people were all born of one common mother, all born on this big Island, wishing to repose under the Tree of Peace and Friendship with all the tribes in the Woods. As God is our witness, we ardently desired that the white and red inhabitants cultivate Brotherly affection and live united by the firmest bands of Love and Friendship....or something like that..."

Button set aside the plucked bird, handing it to the leader, who placed it on a stick and started to roast it.

He turned his attention to skinning the rabbit.

He did an adequate job and stared at the knife, wondering if he could keep it if he showed he was trustworthy.

One Indian had returned. Button didn't even notice he went missing.

Apparently he had been fishing at a nearby stream or pond. Button listened and couldn't hear any water rushing, but he didn't have the refined senses of his captors.

The man took a flat stone and used it

like a trowel to dig up earth. He sliced the fish open and gutted it. With practiced efficiency, he pulled out the skeleton, but he left the scales on.

He encased the fish in clay mud from the ground, which he then threw onto the fire. He repeated the process several times.

Would they be surprised at Button's cooperation, he wondered? Or did they see him as cargo to be sold? Could he demonstrate to them that God Fearing patience does win out? What should he do next? How long was this journey he was on? He didn't know answers, but he knew he had to keep his wits about him.

The men ate and gave him scraps of the meat, as Button expected.

One captor tossed Button a now flame-hardened ball of mud from the fire. Button watched the others to see what he should do next.

They cracked the hot lump open and

out billowed steaming hot cooked fish. The scales had stuck to the sides of the clay. Once it cooled, they took their fingers and scooped out the tender boneless meat.

Button imitated this action and found the fish to be fresh and delicious without any other seasoning.

"Back in August of last year," Button started as he smiled scooping another bit of meat from his clay bowl, "A man named George Washington said 'Perseverance and spirit have done wonders in all ages.' Have you heard the name George Washington?" Button asked looking for a reaction. He repeated, "George Washington?"

The men scooped up dirt and poured it on the fire until it was extinguished. They wiped grease from the cooked meat onto their exposed skin. They cleaned up their area and then shoved Button to let him know which direction they would head.

Again, one man in front, one behind and one on each side of Button. They would walk all day, he supposed.

Button wondered if these men were themselves victims.

Maybe they had land and some sneaky Englishman cheated them out of it, leaving them homeless.

Perhaps they were resentful that the presence of the colonists disrupted their way of life so much.

Perhaps they were simply following orders to collect more shiny trinkets from soldier uniforms. Were they gullibly believing lies spun by loquacious men of business, who paid them in shiny gold buttons.

Was Polly right?

Was there a mastermind orchestrating the kidnapping of colonists for slavery? Button couldn't ask them because...they didn't speak English.

5 CHAPTER 12: (FEB 1776) Will You Investigate?

The doctor made a preliminary examination of Floyd Hargreaves' body, then took a closer look around the room. The window was locked. The door was locked. All locked from the inside of the library.

"Magistrate Pinkney," the doctor called. "Unfortunate as it may be, I would have to assess that Mr. Hargreaves may have taken his own life. His wounds appear to indicate self-murder."

Jane replied, "Well, you must investigate to be sure."

"What is there to investigate, Miss?" Magistrate Pinkney asked, "The room was locked from the inside. The doctor has just said the wounds are consistent with self-murder."

"Well, although I have recently arrived, I do know my Uncle's character and this act is contrary to that character. It is an atrocity, Mr. Pinkney." Jane clarified.

Magistrate Pinkney glanced around the room and walked over to a hutch with glass in the tiny doors. He opened it and extracted a silver menorah, "Was your Uncle Jewish?" He asked.

"What has that to do with..." Bryce Aiden Tyler asked, "He was a very good business..."

Magistrate Pinkney interrupted him, "There is no Jewish synagogue in this area. He may have felt isolated and that could have been a reason for killing himself."

"Nonsense," Jane blurted out. "Just because I was raised at home with two faiths, Christian and Jewish. Neither religion is a reason to kill oneself. Both are loved by God and one can always pray when feeling alone and discouraged. Uncle Floyd's mind was quite sound."

"Then, perhaps, if you say he was killed, then his faith may have been the reason to do away with him. There are some who have hostility against Hebrews," the Magistrate offered.

"Absurd!" Byrce Aiden Tyler stated, "He was a respected honest man of business. Diligent and hard working."

"Success then. Business jealousy could be reason to kill," The doctor offered, "couple that with a different way of worshiping God Almighty and some use that as justification for their actions."

"Then do you say, Sir," Jane started, "That his death was murder and not self-murder?"

The doctor shook his head, "No, it appears to be self-murder. I am sorry my dear, I was simply humoring you as a member of the weaker sex. Your Uncle Floyd must have been hiding his troubles until he could no longer bear the burden of isolation or perhaps he was in great debt."

"Our business was not in debt," Bryce Aiden retorted, "We were quite profitable...but now he is gone...Oh, what am I to do...." He rubbed his head, "I cannot believe his death was due to his Jewish faith."

The magistrate looked around at all those present in the Hargreaves home.

After some silence, Jane stated matter of factly, "The death of my uncle Floyd is an atrocity which must be investigated."

The magistrate took note of those present. There was Jane. Her maid, Silversmith stood next to the butler Witherspoon.

There was this fellow who took the hinges off the door to the library, a former business partner of the deceased, a certain Bryce Aiden Tyler.

There was also a guest of the lady of the house, a tailor, a Mr. Tweedbottom.

The magistrate skipped over the faces of the men who came with him, the doctor and his own brother.

The Magistrate looked directly at Jane and replied, "Atrocity? When our forefathers, the Mayflower pilgrims, landed here more than half of them perished from the weather and illness. Later, others succumbed to a weakened will, loss of love, or animal attacks. I do not think that this," the magistrate pointed to Jane's dead uncle, "that this qualifies as an atrocity. It is sad. It is unfortunate. Now, if you will kindly excuse me, Miss Hargreaves, I will take your Uncle to be properly dealt with. Good day."

With that, he bowed curtly and with a motion, ushered the doctor, and his brother, both of whom were carrying Jane's uncle's body, and walked outside, gently placing the body on the cart.

For a moment, Jane froze, uncertain about what to do.

Then, she turned to her Uncle's business partner, Bryce Aiden Tyler.

"Do you believe Uncle Floyd did away with himself?" Jane asked.

"Your Uncle and I had a recent disagreement, but it was not a matter worthy of shedding blood, Miss Hargreaves," Mr. Tyler replied. "Your uncle is always quite level headed. Was... was level headed... But, the magistrate is simply doing his job."

Determined, Jane snapped, "He can do

his job without being rude," and she marched outside to the cart.

"Mr. Pinkney," Jane called and noticing both Karl Pinkney and his brother turned around, she clarified, "Magistrate, sir."

"Yes, Miss Hargreaves?" the magistrate replied with forced patience.

"Have you men who report to you?" Jane inquired.

"I do, Miss Hargreaves," Magistrate Karl Pinkney replied.

"Then, since you are obviously occupied by other matters, may I request one of your men be instructed to investigate the death of my uncle?" Jane asked with a pleasant smile.

"No, you may not," he replied and started to step up into the cart, himself.

Jane put a hand on his arm to stop him from getting into the cart and said,

"Mr. Pinkney, I don't know what skirmishes or small dust storms occupy your time, but..."

Mr. Tweedbottom had followed Jane outside and now surprised Jane by pulling her hand off the Magistrate. Mr. Tweedbottom apologized to the Magistrate on behalf of Jane.

Mr. Tweedbottom said, "Mr. Magistrate, Sir. I ask your indulgence to excuse Miss Hargreaves. As you know, women don't understand the business nor the politics of men. Yet, she is deluded about her own capability of understanding. You must forgive her for her error in judgement."

Jane turned to Mr. Tweedbottom.

She spoke very slowly, enunciating each syllable clearly, "Would you kindly return inside, Mr. Tweedbottom? Perhaps have another cup of tea?"

The magistrate's brother took a seat in the cart next to the doctor. Jane knew her window of requesting assistance was closing.

Jane turned to the magistrate's brother, who was now closer to her and pleaded,

"Please sir. As the brother of this Magistrate, would you have influence with the rules of this land?"

The magistrate's brother laughed, "I have no influence whatsoever, Miss Hargreaves. That's why I'm helping my brother out with his daily routine."

"I don't quite understand?" Jane replied with a confused quiver.

Mr. Tweedbottom was still standing there. She pointed Mr. Tweedbottom to the door as she requested clarification from the magistrate's brother. Jane was worried that if there was a gap in the conversation, Mr. Tweedbottom might speak, again.

Jane fueled the discussion with, "Please explain the connection between you working with your brother, the magistrate and your degree of influence." Jane smiled as she pushed Mr. Tweedbottom toward the door, beckoning Witherspoon to take him with hand motions.

"Simply put," the magistrate's brother replied, "I'm living with him because he received notice from the Crown to sell all my lands and deposit the money in the King's treasury, else I'd be locked away."

"What?" Jane asked surprised, "Why would King George demand the magistrate's own brother's goods? What offense did you commit?"

Witherspoon collected Mr. Tweedbottom as politely as he could and guided him back into the house.

Now, Mr. Tyler was just coming outside to join the conversation.

The magistrate's brother blurted out a sharp "ha!" before he answered with, "Karl, here is still trying to understand what I've done. Nobody can seem to tell him what crime I have committed. So, until he figures it out, I'm living with him, working with him." He shrugged, "No influence."

The magistrate now broke in, "I have my orders from His Majesty. If I had disobeyed, we both would be in prison. So, that is another matter, which does not concern you, Miss Hargreaves," he replied.

Mr. Tyler now spoke up to the Magistrate, "You mean you had to carry out a punishment against your own brother and neither of you know for what crime he is being punished?"

When Bryce Aiden Tyler got no answer, he continued, "I think that does have a bearing on Miss. Hargreaves' Uncle. If you do not have the authority to learn why your own brother is being punished, then perhaps you do not have the authority to investigate anything, do you?"

"Mr. Tyler," The magistrate started, "Let me assure you that I am the primary investigator of such matters in these parts." He paused and took a breath, "Let me remind you, sir," the magistrate puffed, "Half favor the King. Half favor independence. The natives of this land also aggravate matters. One never knows where a battle may erupt. I must be judicious when assigning my men. Come to me with valid reason to investigate and I will consider it."

Jane added, "Mr. Pinkney. I appreciate how you have trained your brother to be an assistant magistrate of sorts, but the death of my uncle is most definitely out of order and..."

"Miss Hargreaves," Magistrate Pinkney interrupted looking right at Jane with a steely gaze, "I manage order here in these colonies. I happened to be in this town when your maid found me and brought us here. These tiny dust storm skirmishes, as you call them, do indeed take precedence over the issue of a man who killed himself."

"But..." Jane tried to interject.

"Are you friends with any German immigrants, Miss Hargreaves?" he asked.

"No, I've just arrived in the colonies, but that has nothing to..." Jane tried to complete a sentence, again. "Have you heard the name Christopher Seider?" the magistrate persisted.

"Well, no, but..." Jane tried again.

"He was the eleven year old lad, who was the first casualty of political strife. Boston. February 22nd back in 1770. Within a fortnight of his death, there was a massacre in Boston. March fifth."

Jane interjected, "What has that sad affair of six years ago to do with my Uncle's demise today?"

The magistrate replied, "It is my obligation to ensure the safety of the residents within my district. When a man presumes to take his own life, there can be no public outrage and all colonists in my care remain safe."

"So, the boy was murdered," Jane observed.

"Young Mr. Seider," Karl Pinkney replied, "died because he joined a mob bent on harassing a customs service man, who earlier broke up a protest in front of a loyalist shop. The mob threw rocks at his North End home, which broke windows and struck his wife. The owner shot into the crowd. Young Mr. Seider was wounded and died hours later."

"A child perished," Jane commented.

"No. Captain Preston's account said a hundred townsfolk surrounded the house containing the King's money, with the intent of murdering the guard and plundering the chest. This mob was angry over the death of the eleven year old boy. They insulted the dozen soldiers Captain Preston dispatched, with terms such as 'lobster scoundrels' and 'bloody backs'."

"I think a trained soldier would be able to withstand words, Mr. Pinkney," Mr. Tyler added.

The magistrate replied, "Words came to blows. Blows to bayonet. Soldiers were attacked with clubs and snowballs."

"Snowballs? That is no need to fire upon a crowd," Jane added.

The magistrate explained, "According to Preston, the mob yelled 'fire'. It did not. In the subsequent twenty minutes, the confusion was so great soldiers may have fired because they assumed the order came from Preston himself. Sadly, men fell. The King's men had to contain a crowd, which grew to about 5,000. A crowd which beat drums, calling the people to arms in order to kill every soldier present."

"That is horrid," Jane grimaced.

"That is the Bloody Massacre in King Street. And, that is what I call an atrocity. Five. Yes, five, Miss Hargreaves, five common men needlessly died." He took a breath and continued, "I will be reasonable. Here is my offer. When you identify a living soul whose life is threatened, contact me, Miss Hargreaves. Anything less dire than that, and I do not expect to have you calling on me."

The Magistrate seated himself next to his brother and looked straight ahead, ready to depart. Jane and Mr. Tyler stepped back from the horse and cart.

Magistrate Pinkney took a paper out of his breast pocket and handed it to Jane. She accepted it without looking at it. She did not want to break eye contact with Magistrate Karl Pinkney.

The doctor picked up the reins of the horses and with a snap of leather, the horses started to trot off with the three men and the body of Uncle Floyd in the cart.

6 CHAPTER: (FEB 1776) Polly and Mr. Tyler Walk Back Inside

Bryce Aiden Tyler and Jane Hargreaves slowly turned away from the road and walked back inside the house.

Mr. Tweedbottom, curious as usual, asked, "What did the magistrate give you?"

Jane numbly handed the paper to Mr.

Tweedbottom, who took a monocle out of his pocket to read it.

Then with a flippant tone, he said, "He actually had a paper printed up with the addresses of the inns he stays at when making rounds in the towns he manages. How useless."

Mr. Tweedbottom tossed the paper onto the side table and rushed to boldly put an arm around Jane and guide her to the parlor to sit down.

Softly, Mr.Tweedbottom buzzed around Jane like an eager bee ready to pollinate, saying, "Did you see how he challenged the magistrate? That Mr. Tyler is a volatile stormy one. Unpredictable and unsafe. He did not defend and protect you, as I did. I know you cannot think clearly now, My dear Miss Hargreaves. Do come sit with me..."

Bryce Aiden Tyler picked up the paper Mr. Tweedbottom had dismissed and put it into his own pocket. Then, he strode into the library to look at the desk where his business partner had been found dead.

He picked something up, then walked back into the hallway, speaking loudly enough for all to hear, "Miss Hargreaves?" Mr. Tyler started as he walked into the library holding a letter, "Were you aware that your Uncle was invited to a private opera performance by a... singer named Mossop?"

"Opera?" Jane spoke while Mr. Tweedbottom scooted even closer to Jane on the sofa.

Jane summoned the servants and asked, "That letter which Mr. Tyler holds. Did you or Witherspoon bring it in?"

"No, Miss Jane," Silversmith answered, "I did not receive that invitation in person to deliver, nor do I recall it ever having come by post. Your Uncle must have been given the invitation in person at one of his meetings, Miss."

"Oh!" Mr. Tweedbottom blurted out

smiling at Mr. Tyler, ignoring Silversmith and Witherspoon, "Will they play the Music of Colonial from 1735. I mean Boston has been having ballad operas since 1770. It shows great refinement that your Uncle attends a performance in these parts. Even if it is in a home instead of a proper theater. We can prove to the residents of Boston that we are more cultured than they... "

Witherspoon examined the letter held by Mr. Tyler.

Witherspoon replied, "Miss Jane, I was under the impression that your uncle disliked Opera."

Tweedbottom whispered to Jane, "Convenient that Mr. Tyler found that letter, isn't it?"

"Mr.Tweedbottom, I'm conversing with Witherspoon at the moment," Jane replied.

Mr. Tweedbottom slowly pulled away, but still uttering in a barely audible voice,

"Almost as if it weren't there when your Uncle's body was removed...but it is now."

The butler, Witherspoon, continued to speak to Jane, "I am not aware of any meeting Mr. Hargreaves would have had where opera would be a subject. Unlikely he received this note from one of his meetings. I confess that I do not know from whence this letter came." Witherspoon paused and asked Jane, "Would you be considering attending in your uncle's stead?"

Jane turned her attention back to Mr. Tyler, "Uncle Floyd and this opera...Where is this to be?"

"An estate," Mr. Tyler continued as he looked at the paper in his hand, "belonging to a Lady Sarah Wilson? She writes as if she is an intimate friend. Does that name sound familiar to you? Would your uncle have ever gone to Maryland? Rising Sun in Maryland?"

Jane replied, "There are no synagogues

in Maryland." She turned to Bryce Aiden Tyler and added, "Did he not make an agreement with you, Mr. Tyler, that if he moved here to Dover to start the business with you, that should he travel, he would only venture to Colonies with synagogues[1]?"

---

[1] The etymology of the noun **synagogue** refers to the location for regular public worship of Jews. The word comes from Old French *sinagoge*. Modern French *synagogue*. In Late Latin, the word *synagoga* means "congregation of Jews". In Greek, *synagoge* is defined as a "place of assembly" or "meeting," or "a bringing together". Greek translators of the Biblical Old Testament defined late Hebrew *keneseth* as "assembly" or "house of assembly". The word *Knesset* is from Israeli parliament, 1949, from Mishnaic Hebrew *keneseth* meaning "gathering, assembly," stemming from the Hebrew *kanas*, which means "he gathered, assembled, collected."

7 CHAPTER: (MARCH 1776) A Question of Trust

Some days after the death of her Uncle Floyd, Jane found herself pacing about inside the Hargreaves home. "Witherspoon," Jane addressed her butler.

He turned around and replied, "Yes? How might I be of service."

Jane waved the letter Mr. Tyler had found earlier on her Uncle's desk and asked Witherspoon, "Do you trust Mr. Tyler?"

"I have worked for your uncle," the butler replied. "I trust Mr. Hargreaves."

"Indeed, but what of Mr. Tyler?" Jane persisted.

"...I would say perhaps," the butler clarified. "You see I know Mr. Tyler has been forthright in business with Mr. Hargreaves, however I cannot suppose what lurks in his heart. All I can say with certainty is that I trust the judgement of Mr. Hargreaves and he trusted Mr. Tyler."

"Hmmm..." Jane started, "This invitation to the opera... I need you to hire a driver for me, Witherspoon. How quickly can you fetch some candidates? "

8 CHAPTER 15: (MARCH 1776) To Hire

It took some days, however, before Witherspoon was able to select candidate drivers to meet Jane's specifications. She had demanded that as much scrutiny be applied to the driver's character as the ability to actually drive a carriage. She might, after all, need to employ this man for some time.

At last, Witherspoon, approached Jane. "Miss Jane," the Butler started, "As you requested, I have searched and believe I have found a suitable driver. His name is Mr. Billy Dawes. He would be able to take you and Silversmith to the Wilson Estate for the opera performance."

"Do tell me of him," Jane said to Witherspoon. "Are his qualifications sound?"

"Yes, Miss Jane." The butler cleared his throat. "The townsfolk say he can easily drive a cart in Springtime, when the roads are the most muddy and uneven."

"Does he keep company with layabouts or skilled disciplined men?" Jane asked.

Witherspoon replied, "Mr. Dawes is acquainted with a Mr. Paul Revere, also an excellent horseman and other similarly skilled disciplined men."

"And, what of his skills?" Jane asked.

"Mr. Dawes," Witherspoon shared, "Is adept with managing carriages with up to six horses. He also has a sleigh he can use in winter when the roads are laden with smooth snow. He received his training in Massachusetts Bay, where as you know, carriages were in use for the last century, since the 1680's."

"So, Witherspoon," Jane thoughtfully added, "This Mr. Dawes is adept with conditions of roads... but what of his ability to brave rough terrain with unsavory natives?" Jane asked, "We must plan for every event. This is not London."

"I have confirmed," Witherspoon replied, "Mr. Billy Dawes has delivered mail on horseback to Postmaster William Watson. To do that requires covering over 60 miles of rough roads between Cambridge and Sandwich. This terrain requires great caution and the trek would take hours. He appears to be inventive. Mr. Dawes suggested that the Postmaster use a stage coach instead of horseback, which would allow for more mail to be carried. But of course to do that, the roads would first need to be..." The butler trailed off.

"So," Jane cleared her throat, "is he from a family of drivers, then? Or one of these stable boys who fancies he can take a lady on a long journey just because he knows how to brush a horse or pick a hoof?" Jane was becoming nervous about embarking to an unknown estate and presenting herself as a substitute guest for her uncle. She wanted to be quite sure of her hire.

"I confess I know little of his lineage," Witherspoon added. "But perhaps some local history will quell your concerns."

"History?" Jane asked confused.

"Mr. Dawes told me his Grandfather helped to establish the postal buildings which used fixed postage rates. This was in 1691. Thomas Neale received the North American Postal Service Grant, which helped to establish those postal buildings."

"Where did Mr. Dawes' grandfather accomplish this?"

"In the Virginian and Massachusetts colonies," Witherspoon replied.

"What does he do to earn his income presently?" Jane inquired.

"Mr. Billy Dawes," Witherspoon stated, "Works mostly for news printers to help deliver papers. Last year, sometime in July of 1775, Mr. Dawes worked under that system Benjamin Franklin decreed and William Goddard managed."

"System? What system?" Jane prodded.

"The one which established a formal delivery system for a new postal service to improve upon the Crown Post." Witherspoon paused, "Would Mr. Dawes be an acceptable driver, or shall I continue the search for another candidate?"

"No, no," Jane replied, "This fellow's credentials do seem sufficient. Do hire him and have him bring his carriage around here. I shall ask Silversmith to finish packing. Thank you."

Jane left the room. Witherspoon walked into the kitchen and smiled at Silversmith. "Did you find a driver for Miss Jane?" Silversmith asked Witherspoon.

"Yes. Mr. Billy Dawes. I'm to engage him." Witherspoon sat down. "The house will be quite empty..." Witherspoon's voice trailed off.

Silversmith walked to Witherspoon, "I will write to you. I don't know how long we will be gone. It could be a couple of days or several months. I'm taking most of Miss Jane's clothes, you see... just in case. She really wants to find out what happened to Mr. Hargreaves."

"I understand. I wish I could help in some..." Witherspoon replied, "I could mend that uneven chair leg...or polish the silver...or..."

"Well, you could make the place inviting for when we return...or I'm sure there are some business needs that Mr. Tyler will still require..." Silversmith looked down, then placed a hand on his shoulder, "you could visit your friend at the other household...and I promise to write. I will write..."

"I would appreciate that, Silversmith," Witherspoon sighed. "I would appreciate that very much."

Silversmith lowered her voice to Witherspoon, "You don't need to look for another job, Witherspoon. If Miss Jane's allowance won't cover your salary, she'll devise a way to make some money to keep you. You do not need to look for another position. And...I will write..."

Unbeknownst to Silversmith and Witherspoon, Jane was just outside the Kitchen, listening quietly behind the wall. Jane took a deep controlled breath.

A tear welled up and trickled down her check. She stepped carefully away so as to avoid making noise and headed back upstairs to her bed chamber.

Was she re-living what she had left behind in England? Another family member dead. Would Uncle Floyd's passing away leave her even more destitute?

Would she lose Silversmith this time in this New World?

Silversmith was right. Jane was determined. Determined to do the right thing. She owed it to her Uncle Floyd to find out why he died; owed it to him to find out what he was working on and finish it for him.

Then, she could worry about her own affairs.

Once inside her bedroom, she walked directly to a doll which had been hers since childhood.

She turned it upside down and opened up a hidden pocket. She reached inside to extract a handful of gold coins. Then, she turned the doll right side up and placed it back on the shelf. It was time to stop playing with dolls and be an adult.

Jane was intending to save up money for her first 'made in the colonies' dress. The one she planned to order from Mr. Tweedbottom.

Now, she determined to use the gold to pay Mr. Billy Dawes, the driver, as well as Witherspoon, the butler, and of course Silversmith and whatever expenses they might incur on this trip. She would use this money to investigate what really happened to Uncle Floyd.

She slipped the coins into her skirt pocket.

If it turned out to be self murder after all, she would have to accept that shameful fact and acknowledge she would be the subject of gossip.

If it was murder, she would want to see the guilty party punished.

Either way, the course of action she was about to undertake would taint her eligibility to enter certain social circles.

Jane sat down on her bed. She had to accept that. Not only would she not be able to afford the right sort of lace or other measures of high station, but this search for the truth might be considered...vulgar and unlady-like in manner.

And would Mr. Tweedbottom, with his exacting tastes wish to marry her, then? "Probably not," Jane said aloud to herself.

She took a deep slow breath, "Life is changing anyway. I might as well give it a bit of a push ahead."

She stood up and walked to the window to gaze out on the happenings in town.

"In the colonies, one doesn't need to marry, anyway. One only needs to determine how to make enough money to keep the staff employed, as Silversmith said I would do..." she whispered.

She sighed and looked at her childhood doll and asked, "But how am I going to do that?

9 CHAPTER 16: (MARCH 1776) Billy Dawes' Carriage Ride

"Silversmith, are you ready?" Jane asked from inside the foyer

Billy Dawes, her new driver, was finishing loading Jane Hargreaves' luggage on top of the carriage. The horses looked strong and healthy.

Mr. Dawes nodded to Witherspoon to let him know that the carriage was ready to accept passengers. Witherspoon, outside with mister Dawes, now opened the front door to allow the ladies to come outside and enter the carriage.

"Yes, Miss Jane," Silversmith started, "I'm ready."

The two women walked out the front door and outside past Witherspoon who stood alone to wish them *bon voyage*.

Jane stopped and turned to Witherspoon while Silversmith was helped into the carriage by Mr. Dawes.

"Witherspoon," Jane started, "I don't know how long this journey will take, but I want you to know that I am planning on coming back and I do hope you will be here when I return."

A bit surprised, Witherspoon replied, "Thank you, Miss Hargreaves. I wish you a safe and productive journey."

Jane slipped Witherspoon some money, "That is to pay you in advance...just in case this takes a while."

"Thank you, Miss Hargreaves," Witherspoon was tempted to refuse the money, but being practical overruled his initial instinct and he accepted it.

He continued with concerned deference, "I shall be here should you need me. I have taken the liberty of speaking to Mr. Dawes about ensuring your safety on this journey. He informed me he slept solidly so that he could ride throughout the night and get you to your location by morning. A moving carriage will deter thieves wishing to attack."

"Well done, Witherspoon. One cannot be too cautious." Jane forced a smile, "Let us find out why my Uncle who hates opera was invited in such a familiar manner by a woman none of us ever heard of, shall we?" Jane took a long look back at her Uncle Floyd's home.

Then, Jane was helped inside the carriage by Mr. Dawes.

Jane leaned her head against the seat inside the carriage, closing her eyes.

Mr.Dawes took control of the horses and the coach lurched forward. Silversmith looked out the window on the side of the carriage and waved good bye to Witherspoon, who awkwardly waved in response.

The wooden wheels beneath the carriage bumped along.

Jane vowed never to tell Silversmith she overheard her conversation with Witherspoon. She wouldn't have to.

She would get answers, find a source of income, and continue to live her life in these colonies. This New World was her new home. There was nothing to go back to in England.

After some time, Jane's upright position made her squirm in her corset. She could not lean back at a comfortable angle.

The only position where her back did not hurt after hours of travel was to sit straight up. To do that, one must remain awake. The repetition of the rhythmic clomps of the horses hooves did eventually lull Jane to sleep, unable to keep her eye lids open.

Mr. Dawes, as Witherspoon told Jane earlier, did ride the carriage and horses through the night.

Jane was sleeping peacefully until she realized Silversmith was shaking her awake.

Jane looked out the window as they were slowly stopping. It was still dark, probably early morning by now.

Why were they slowing down?

Groggily, Jane saw Silversmith's face illuminated by a shaft of moonlight. Silversmith wore a look of panic.

Then, their carriage jerked to a halt, pitching Silversmith and Jane forward. Jane heard Billy Dawes outside yell, "Whoa. Whooooaaaaaa."

They were surrounded by wilderness. They were not at their destination.

Jane asked Silversmith, "Why are we stopping?"

10 CHAPTER 17: (MARCH 1776) Day Two and Two Shots Heard

Button Gwinette, captive of four Indian men, walked and walked and walked.

The leader, the one with the tokens from soldier uniforms strung around his neck like a mantel of bravery, would occasionally shake his necklace to the others, as if to reinforce his position as leader and emphasize the urgency of this mission.

Button wondered if each brass button or shiny gold coin represented a kidnapped colonist.

The leader would turn around and notice one of the men getting tired.

He would stop and shake his necklace at the tired man and that would work to get the company moving again.

"Determination, eh?" Button said once to the leader, "Are we marching onward to indulge the greedy pleasures of some entitled merchant? Or King?" Button smiled, wondering if any words would be recognized.

The leader replied, "You drink."

Button nodded and trudged onward, "I have never opposed King George. Taking me is a mistake. I'm English and His Majesty and I are friends..."

Button looked for a reaction and got none.

Button wondered what his fate would be. Would he be handed over to the women of a tribe and be tortured for sport until dead?

Would he be packed tightly with hundreds of other slaves to be shipped off to some foreign land, never again to see his Polly?

Would he be used in a hostage exchange to free one of their prisoners?

Would he be scalped so that his hairline could be sold for more trinkets to add to the leader's necklace?

Was this a case of mistaken identity? Perhaps they meant to take somebody else? Was this really happening to other colonists as himself?

On they walked. On and on. For hours...

Then, all five, Button and his four captors, stopped at a clearing. This clearing was near a pond of fresh water.

One of his captors pointed to a pile of sticks, walked over, grabbed one and then placed it in the middle of the clearing. Apparently, the group was going to set up a camp fire and it was up to Button to gather the wood.

Button smiled and did as he was instructed.

They had too many sliced cutting devices for button to attempt escape. Knives, sharpened bones, tomahawks, arrows...too many things to throw at or shoot at Button should he run.

Two men left. Two men stayed. With Button.

Button gathered firewood from around the clearing, piling sticks up. Button assumed the men who left went to hunt. One of the men who stayed gave him a bowl and pointed to the pond. Button filled it up. He also drank some water while he was there.

Then, the man beat several branches of an oak tree and out fell acorns. He took the acorns and put them in the water and put the bowl on the fire. He was going to boil the acorns.

Button reasoned that the acorns must have an acidic or astringent property about them. He knew when he ate astringent foods, he would get an ache in his stomach and his mouth would pucker. But, when boiled that astringency was removed making it safe to eat.

Later, those men returned and did bring back a kill. Birds they had shot with arrows. Button again wondered how he could escape if his captors were such excellent marksmen.

It was Button's task to pluck the feathers.

When he finished the first bird, he handed it to one of the men. He wanted them to start the fire so he could singe off the quills from the bird he plucked, but there was no way he could ask them to do that.

That captor took a flint-edged knife and sliced the bird in a quick an expert manner. He made it look so easy. Then the man looked at Button. Button looked away. He wouldn't want this man to move from slicing up the bird to slicing Button's scalp off.

Button's hands started to get slippery from plucking out the feathers. Each quill, once plucked, would leave a dent in the skin, which would ooze just a little bit onto his hands.

When he and Polly would shoot down fowl and prepare the bird to eat, they would pull out the large feathers. Then they would take fire and singe off any quills which remained in the skin.

Another man started a fire with the sticks Button gathered earlier. Button took a small stick of fire and used it to singe off the quills. The men looked suspicious at first. They watched him for some time, curious about his actions. When they saw he was simply preparing the bird to be roasted, they left Button alone.

After the bird was roasted, the men ate.

The boiled acorns in the pot of water were ready and the men took the now mushy acorns and ate them, as well.

An eagle flew overhead. Button watched it soar, majestically slicing the sky with a whisper in the azure blue. Blue. The color of freedom . The Red Coats used a dye created from white ground up dried cochineal bugs scraped off the cacti pads found in warm climates. Button wondered why they chose red. Perhaps to cover up the splashes of blood incurred in battle. Red. It did not serve as camouflage in nature...not like blue...

Button pushed a bird onto a stick and stuck it in the fire. The smell of the crisping skin and blaze of flame surging with every drop of fat which fell onto the flame, made Button hungry

As before, the men devoured the roasted meat, first. Then, the men rubbed the grease from the cooked meats into their own skin and with full stomachs, they lay down on their blankets

What was left over was given to Button to consume.

After they all had eaten, Button was directed into the center of the circle, near the smoldering fire. The men set out blankets to sleep on. They pushed Button into a spot for him to lie down.

As before, they put a blanket on top of Button. One man would lay down on either side of him, locking him in, pinning him to the earth. Button deduced this must be how they guarded their captives each night while also getting rest, themselves. Button assumed this ritual would occur each night until they reached their destination.

Once again, Button soon heard the deep breathing of his two captors sleeping next to him. Then, the two men near the fire across the campsite began to snore.

In the distance, he heard the sounds of wildlife. All was peaceful. Then, he heard a pop and an echo across the valley.

Was that a gun firing?

He looked around. All his captors were asleep. It was distant, but it sounded familiar.

Button held his breath.

Would there be more shots? Was the shooter reloading?

He listened. Moments passed and he heard nothing. He waited and looked around to see if any of his captors awoke.

They remained deep in slumber. He closed his eyes and took a deep breath. Then, he heard another shot.

Button started to groan as if he were suffering from a stomach ache, an idea which formed once he saw the astringent acorns. He jerked his legs as much as he could under the blanket which hampered his movements.

He was determined his captors would not have a peaceful slumber.

11 CHAPTER 18: (MARCH 1776) Polly and the Wild Attack

Polly was so exhausted she didn't realize she had actually fallen asleep .

When she awoke, the dusk was fading into darkness. Polly was surprised so much time had passed. Only when a bird flew by her still body did she suddenly awaken. The fowl cawed a God-given warning.

The chill of night was settling in and she could feel the dank air was much colder now. One of her hands had fallen in her empty basket, now covered with a gooey broken egg. The raw eggs had cracked earlier, she remembered. Some egg fell as she was running. Others served as slimy nourishment when Polly needed something to eat.

Polly was just collecting her thoughts, planning her next move when she felt a lick on her fingers.

Her heart raced and she involuntarily gasped, then held her breath. Eyes wide, she turned her head slowly to see what had licked her hand.

In the shaft of moonlight, she saw a tiny piglet had wandered toward her and started to lick the broken egg from her fingers.

She was unaware of the warm tongue until she saw another little piglet. At first, she was frightened, then she smiled at the tiny creatures... and then she slowly realized if these tiny piglets were here, where was the protective and ferocious mother.

These piglets were so precious. Polly had accidentally disturbed a farrow of piglets. Polly preferred waking to these tiny forest creatures than to any savage attackers.

If the ones who raided her cabin had been searching for her, they would have found her by now. She sighed.

Her husband Button could well have given up his life to protect hers and their unborn babe. But, there was a chance he could have survived. A slender chance is still a chance.

Satisfied she was not being pursued, Polly listened to the forest surrounding her. She wondered if the mother of these piglets might be nearby. Polly slowly drew her hand away and wiped her hand on her skirts.

No sounds of gunfire. No sounds of fighting. No sound of a mother sow. No other motion. All seemed quiet.

She looked up to the sky to get her bearings from the stars. The tree branches obscured the evening canopy. Polly was determined to travel during the night so she could get to a town, but she didn't know in which direction to head.

Polly slowly pushed away a little piglet and got to her knees, but she accidentally hit the tail on another piglet, which squealed. Instinctively she touched her own belly. Maybe she'd nickname her child piglet. No. That would be silly.

She used the sturdy handle of the basket as a crutch and started to get to her knees. Suddenly, a twig snapped behind her.

Cautiously, still on her knees, she turned her head toward the sound.

In a shaft of moonlight, in a small clearing just past some fallen trees which formed a three-foot-tall barrier before her, she saw a stout dark sparsely haired 300 pound creature with a snout and two curved tusks and it was staring right at her.

It stared right at Polly who was kneeling too close to the wild boar's farrow of piglets; and Polly had made the piglet squeal, which must have alerted its mother.

Slowly and without challenging eye contact, she stood upright while placing one hand slowly inside her pocket to retrieve the firearm Button had insisted she carry.

With her hand covered in sticky piglet saliva and egg yolk, the butt of the weapon slipped around preventing her from grasping it firmly.

Polly sucked in a deep breath and suddenly bolted away from the boar.

Polly didn't know if this was just a single wild pig, or if this beast came from a sounder of pigs, which could be nearby.

Polly couldn't contend with a sounder of mature wild boars. She hoped all she had to deal with was this one mother pig and her farrow of piglets.

Foolishly, Polly tried to outrun this wild beast, which easily leapt over a hedge, clearing it by a of couple feet. The hairs on the angry boar's shoulders were upright. Tail stood straight up like a soldier carrying a flag into battle. From her gullet came a distinct growl.

Polly instantly recalled her husband telling her that these creatures had kept pace with a galloping horse. She realized, she could not out run the beast.

Polly had to stop running, turn, stand, and fight.

But, then Polly tripped and fell onto painful shards of bark and rock, cutting the palm of her hand. She yelped in pain.

When confronted with Polly's jarring piercing screams, the wild pig became aggravated.

In the blink of an eye, Polly rolled onto her back, her palms scraped and bleeding from the fall.

She stared straight up at the bright moon noting she found a clearing where she could finally see all the stars, but that image was eclipsed by the black mass flying over her head.

The boar had sprung up about five feet, and was about to land with mouth open, ready to bite this invader of the piglet litter. Drool dripped from her curved tusks, which glistened in the moonlight.

Without being able to withdraw her revolver she found the trigger while the firearm remained in the pocket of her skirts. She aimed up and shot once.

The pig squealed and landed on top of Polly.

Polly gasped at the sudden weight being dropped on her. With much effort, she groaned with all her might as she pushed, inch by inch, the breathing beast off her.

It was still alive and only stunned. To her surprise, the boar became active again and started biting her skirts, searching for her leg to clamp onto. Her other leg was pinned by the weight of this creature.

It's sharp tusk scraped Polly's flesh, drawing blood. Yet, Polly managed to free her leg as the pig re-positioned itself. Polly pushed herself onto her hands and knees to face this attacker.

Polly withdrew her flintlock with one hand and a lead ball in her other pocket with the other hand.

Only one shot remained as the other lead balls fell out on the ground during her struggles. She grabbed the pouch of gun powder and tried to pour it in.

Realizing she needed time to load, she found her basket, ripping a stiff bit of straw from the handle, she then tossed it to the side to distract the beast. This caused the pig to look at the flying object, but nothing more.

Polly didn't have a ramrod to shove down the barrel, so she held the stock and took the stiff straw she had pulled from the handle and used that to pack the lead ball and powder.

Instantly, the boar's attention returned to Polly.

In the few seconds she had, Polly got the lead ball into the chamber of her firearm. The low growls of this mother pig elicited high-pitched squeals from the piglets nearby.

Then, Polly's last remaining bullet tumbled out of the chamber.

Still on her knees, Polly dropped the firearm and picked up a nearby branch with both hands, swinging at the pigs snout to keep it distant.

She recalled somewhere that if one smacks the nose of a cat, it would sneeze and she hoped this technique might cause the boar to act likewise. With all her might, she did strike the snout of the beast. This, she found, to be a useless ineffectual maneuver.

She located a rock and threw it at the beast's head, stunning it.

As she turned to get up, her hand fell onto the shape of a lead ball, so she remained on her knees.

She grasped the lead ball. It could have been the one which had rolled out of its chamber, or perhaps one of the many balls which had scattered earlier when she was locked in this pig battle. It happened to be next to the flintlock she dropped earlier.

While returning the lead-ball to where it would be more useful, she saw the pig, slightly wounded, was more eager than ever to engage her.

A beam of moonlight shone through the shifting clouds above to provide just enough light for Polly to confirm the ball was in place. She held the loaded flintlock with shaking hands.

The grunting creature boldly stepped closer. Polly turned to see the determined beady eyes glitter like iced frost mingled with a haunting determination to pounce. Polly wondered if any of the wounds she had inflicted on this pig would slow it down.

Then one of the piglets squealed a particularly loud cry and the mother turned aside to look, turning broadside, exposing the heart and lungs.

Finally, the distraction Polly needed. She started to aim her firearm at this vulnerable area of the pig.

Before she could pull the trigger, the boar had turned back to Polly.

Polly, still on her hands and knees, stretched out her arm holding the weapon as the boar opened its mouth and jumped toward her.

Polly's muzzle touched the bristling throat of the beast as it leapt over her head. With eyes closed, Polly squeezed the trigger with a loud BANG.

Three hundred pounds of dead weight slammed on top of Polly's shoulders, flattening her face down into the forest floor.

Hot blood spurted from the pig's neck. Polly lay motionless, uncertain.

The beast did not move.

Hoping it must be dead, Polly started the excruciating task of trying to push the weight of the beast off her.

She could not lay there with a dead bloody animal pinning her down. She would simply become a meal for yet another hunting predator.

Before her was a low branch hanging from a tree. She grabbed it.

She dragged herself forward, scraping against the ground.

Slowly she eased her way out from under the animal.

Once her legs were freed, the beast rolled onto her skirts.

With a yank, Polly ripped her skirts free and with all her muscles exhausted, Polly panted as she struggled to regain her balance.

Dizzy, and with skirts torn and drenched in blood, Polly realized she could not stop and rest.

Nevertheless, Polly had to force one foot in front of the other with deliberate and conscious moves. She had to find civilization, lest she be attacked again.

Wobbly, she looked up into the face of the full moon above her.

In a few hours, it would be morning. She should be able to cover some ground by then.

Feeling ill, she looked back at the dead animal which had just attacked her. She didn't want to kill.

This pig was acting as a protective mother. Polly would probably act the same way about her own child, if she felt it was threatened.

Then, the piglets started squealing, again. Polly limped away, still hearing them as their cries faded.

After some moments, in the moonlight, Polly squinted. She stepped out with her left foot and felt something flat and free of vegetation beneath the soles of her shoe.

Was this a road?

She stepped on it with her right foot, but her ankle became tangled in the mesh of roots, branches and stones which littered the area.

She lost her balance.

She wavered, trying to regain her footing, but once her head hit the ground, she was unconscious.

12 What Just Happened?

Polly was forced from her home and her husband by an attack. As she sought shelter in the forests, she encountered yet another sort of attack from a wild beast.

Confronted with exhaustion compounded by her already delicate state, she summoned up all her wits to confront and fight back. But, now she is dazed, exhausted, and wonders if only peril awaits her in the future.

Meanwhile, Jane has realized that she cannot go back to England. These rag-tag colonies are her new home, yet her Uncle was her only sure protector and guide. Now that he is gone, the burden falls upon her shoulders. She must now find the truth in an unfair and unformed society. As she seeks to secure her own well being, moved by her recent loss and emboldened by her desire to be the provider to her uncle's household, she unknowingly places herself in jeopardy and even danger. Whom can she trust? Who is her ally and who is her foe?

13 Did You Know...

History of **Lorgnette**: A lorgnette is a spectacle on a short handle, which resembles a stick. The original design of a spectacle was to pinch the bridge of the nose. Early designs did not have arms to rest over your ears. The French used the word 'lorgnette' as early as the 17th century to describe a spyglass (small telescope). Some spyglasses also had handles, similar to a lorgnette. The French word for what we call a lorgnette is actually *face-a-main.*

The lorgnette is believed to have been invented around 1770 by George Adams the 1st (1709-1772). His son wrote "Essay on Vision" (1789 and again in 1792). The Lorgnette was described as a substitute for spectacles.

14 Vocabulary

In the early 1770s, before the colonies united into the United States of America, some words and terms were used, which may be explained in this section.

Jest: A joke. Talking with good-natured fun. To speak in a playful way.

Etching: The art of making designs on metal, glass, etc. by using acid. The picture or figure made this way is also called an etching.

Quaint: Charming in an old fashioned way.

Repute: Public respect. Good name. Reputation.

Self-aggrandizement: When a person boasts or brags. Try to increase one's own power or wealth.

ABOUT THE AUTHOR

Wynter Sommers is the pseudonym for an American writing team. The team consists of technology specialists, PhD's, and other field-tested experts.

With over thirty years of in-classroom experience, the authors artistically weave subtle meaning into each narrative to lend lasting appeal to this new classic, which encourages repeated readings.

By pursuing an enjoyable fictional adventure, the reader learns of many educational topics and hones skills in US History, reading comprehension, critical thinking, social studies and more.

Each time a story theme is explored, new meaning is revealed. Objective facts in the "Did you know" section stimulate conversation, provoking heartfelt introspection on various topics.

Everyday characters in extraordinary situations, demonstrate the value of choosing a real-life action of peace, honor, integrity, truth, patience and perseverance to overcome obstacles in real life. Wynter Sommers hopes each tale inspires action, creativity, and kindness towards your neighbor. One never knows when a small choice today will impacted generations into the future.

Choose wisely.

True love is the toughest substance on earth. Wynter Sommers hopes you will enjoy the other BJORN ESTERDAY WAS NOT BORN YESTERDAY stories in this series.